The Illustrated Book of Aesop's Fables

AESOP

WAS A GREEK SHEPHERD

WHO, MORE THAN 2,500 YEARS AGO,

TOLD STORIES ABOUT

THE LIVES AND BEHAVIORS

OF PEOPLE, OFTEN

USING ANIMALS AS

HEROES.

Aesop's fables continue to be popular today. That's why this book and its wonderful illustrations will be so much fun for you.

In THE ILLUSTRATED BOOK OF AESOP'S FABLES we have chosen four animals as main characters: a fox, a wolf, an eagle, and a lion. Each animal participates in seven fables with other animals or, sometimes, with a person. By talking about everyday situations that animals experience, Aesop shows human defects and virtues.

Aesop wanted to say: We should not look down on those who are smaller or inferior because someday they may be the only ones who can help or save us ("A lion and . . . a mouse"). Patience is the remedy and the solution in many situations ("A fox and . . . another who ate a lot"). True friends never harm each other ("An eagle and . . . a fox"). Truth always triumphs ("A wolf and . . . a sheep"). These are some examples of the attitudes that people should have toward others that you'll find in this book.

CONTENTS

A fox and . . .

A wolf and . . .

An eagle and . . .

A lion and . . .

A fox and . . .

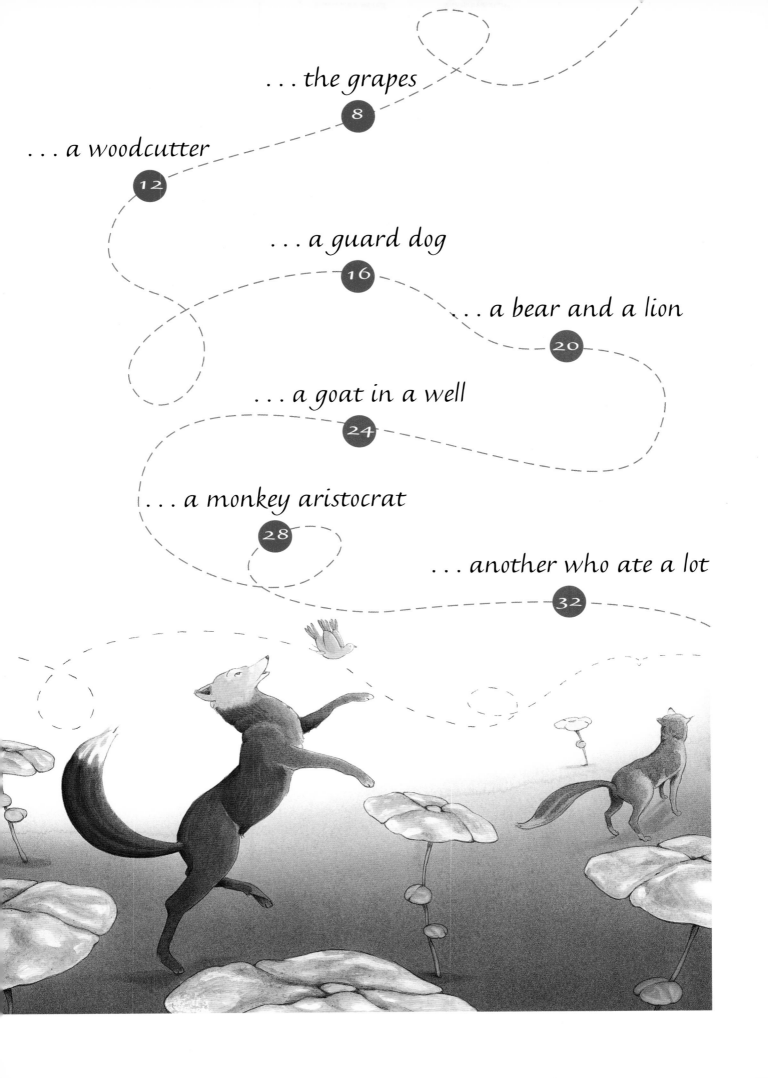

A fox and ...
the grapes

A fox was walking through an orchard that was full of
fruit trees and grapevines loaded with delicious-looking
bunches of ripe muscatel grapes.

One of the vines was heavy with particularly enormous, appetizing bunches of grapes, and the fox, whose mouth watered from just looking at them, began circling around them, jumping higher and higher, trying to reach the brightest, most beautiful bunch.

Her first leaps were just practice. After that, she began bouncing up and down. She tried jumping from different angles, taking a running start. She kept on for a long time, but her front paws—and much less her mouth, her tongue, or her teeth—never even came close to a single grape.

Worn out, but without losing the pride that is so typical of those who are used to getting what they want, the fox walked off angrily, looking back at the grapes out of the corner of her eye, and with her head held high she announced to anyone who might chance to hear:

"Bah, how stupid! I don't like those grapes at all. They're little and dirty and sour and besides that . . . they're still green!"

And with her nose in the air, she left the orchard.

If the fox had been sincere, she would have admitted that she was too small to reach the grapes; she would not have said they were bad. It is better to recognize our own defects and not put the blame on others.

A fox and . . .
a woodcutter

Some hunters had been chasing a fox through the forest for hours
while she ran and ran in search of a place to hide.

In a clearing in the woods she came upon a woodcutter's house and
begged him to let her hide inside. He told her to go in and wait.

Almost immediately the hunters arrived and asked the
woodcutter if he had seen any foxes nearby.

He told them no, he had not seen the fox, but at the same time he pointed at his house to let them know that the animal was there.

The hunters did not understand his gesture, and they went away, since the woodcutter had told them in words that he had not seen a fox.

When the hunters were gone, the fox, who had heard what the woodcutter said and also understood quite well what he meant to tell them with his hands, walked away without saying good-bye. This made the woodcutter angry, and he criticized her for leaving without thanking him for having saved her life.

But the fox, very dignified, answered in this way: "I would thank you if your gestures had been as sincere as your words."

We must be sincere in both what we say and what we do. We should not do what the woodcutter did, say one thing and do the opposite.

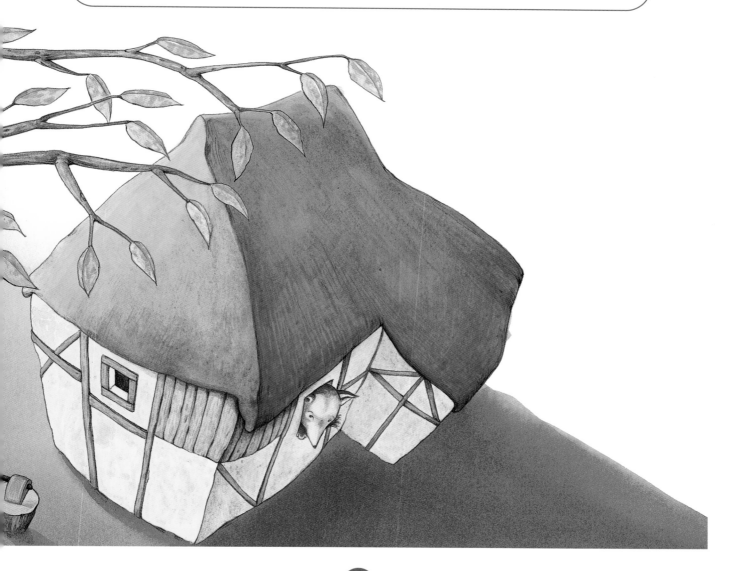

A fox and . . .
a guard dog

In a wide valley that nestled in the hills like a soft green cloak, a large herd of sheep was grazing, with many young lambs among them. They were all munching the fresh grass when a fox managed to slip into the herd without the sheepdogs seeing her.

The fox selected a little lamb only a few days old and, to win his confidence, began licking and petting him and talking to him sweetly.

Just when the fox was beginning to feel very happy at the success of her trick, one of the dogs whose task it was to guard the herd stepped up to her and asked her straight out:

"What are you doing, you foolish thing? Don't you know your own customs, and the customs of the sheep and lambs? And don't you know what I am here for?"

"I'm only caressing and playing with him," answered the fox, trying to look innocent.

"Well, leave him alone right now if you don't want me
to tear you apart with my finest caresses."

And the fox let the little lamb go and ran off with
her tail between her legs.

We should watch the people around us closely, and then we will know
who wishes us well and who might hurt us.

A fox and …
a bear and a lion

A fawn got tangled up in the brambles of the forest and in a little while it died. Just at that moment a big bear and a hungry lion saw it there at the same time and they both jumped to carry it off.

When neither one succeeded in doing that, they decided to fight one another to decide who would end up keeping the fawn.

They fought on and on without a moment's rest. The bear growled while his claws dug into the lion and the lion roared while he clawed at the bear, and the little fawn lay on the ground close by the two fighters.

A fox who was passing by saw that the two fierce beasts were almost exhausted by their struggle, while their prey lay there off to one side. Without thinking twice she rushed past the two animals, picked up the body of the fawn, and calmly carried it off with her.

"How silly we've been! What terrible luck. Such an effort, such a struggle, such a fierce battle . . . and all for the fox to carry off the prize! We would have been better off sharing what could have been our meal today!"

Each of them wanted it all for himself . . . and both the bear and the lion ended up going hungry. They would have come out ahead if they had shared what they had.

A fox and . . .
a goat in a well

One day a fox leaned over the edge of a well near a country house to drink some water, and she fell in. And since the well was quite deep, she couldn't get out again, no matter how hard she tried. After a little while a goat came to the well with the same idea in mind and, when he saw the fox, asked her if the water was good.

Without admitting she had fallen in, she told him that the well water was marvelous—cool and crystal clear—and invited him to come down to where she was to taste the delicious water.

Without thinking twice about it, the goat jumped into the well and, after satisfying his thirst, he asked her what they had to do to get out of there.

Then the fox proposed a plan.

"There is a way that will certainly save us. Put the hooves of your front legs high up against the wall and stretch the horns on your head up as far as you can. I'll climb up your back and once I'm out, I'll pull you out after me."

The goat believed her and did just as she had suggested. In this way the fox managed to get out of the well. As soon as she was out of it she walked off without doing anything to help the goat.

When the goat, shouting as loud as he could, begged her to keep her promise, the fox came back, leaned over the edge of the well and said:

"My dear friend, if you had as much SENSE as you have hairs in your beard, you would not have climbed down into the well without first thinking about how to get out afterward."

Before you start something, you have to think about how you will finish. It did not occur to the goat that after going down into the well he would have to get out of it.

A fox and ...
a monkey aristocrat

Two companions, a fox and a monkey, were traveling the world, and as they walked they talked and eventually began to argue on the subject of the nobility of their families and their family trees.

The fox was proud of having famous kin and great heroes among her ancestors, and the monkey boasted to his traveling companion of exactly the same thing.

Each one was describing in detail the exploits of their ancestors when they came to a spot where the monkey suddenly stopped. It was a cemetery with beautiful marble tombs and immense sculptures. The monkey, standing there before all those tombs, burst out crying inconsolably and began to make excited, exaggerated leaps into the air.

The fox, a bit surprised, asked him what the matter was. The monkey, still crying, showed her the most beautiful tombs and said:

"How do you expect me not to cry, when I am standing in front of the funeral monuments of those great heroes who were my ancestors?"

"You can lie as much as you want!" the fox answered. "You can say that these dead people are your grandparents, your uncles, cousins, or even brothers or parents, because none of them can stand up and deny it!"

And the fox preferred to continue on her way alone.

It is impossible for people not to discover our lies sooner or later. You can catch a liar faster than you can catch a one-legged man.

A fox and ...
another who ate a lot

One day at about noon, in a field where there were many great oak
trees, a fox was searching for food because she had not eaten
anything for several days. She was terribly hungry and could
not find anything to satisfy her hunger.

By chance it happened that while sniffing at a hole in the trunk of
an old oak tree she found some big pieces of roast meat and fresh
baked bread that some shepherds had left hidden there.

The hungry fox had no difficulty climbing into the hole in the tree.
Once inside she began her feast. She ate until she was stuffed.
What a pleasure it was!

But she had eaten so much that her stomach grew big,
and when she wanted to climb out of the hole in the
trunk of the oak, it was impossible.

She tried all sorts of ways of getting out, but she could not fit
through the hole. She began to feel desperate and started to cry.

Another fox who was passing by heard her cries and asked what
the matter was. When she heard the whole story, the second fox said:

"Oh, dear sister! Keep calm, stay in there and be very patient. In a few days you will surely be thin again, and then you will be able to climb out with no problem at all!"

Whoever wants everything, loses all.
Eating a lot . . . will give you a stomach ache.

A wolf and . . .

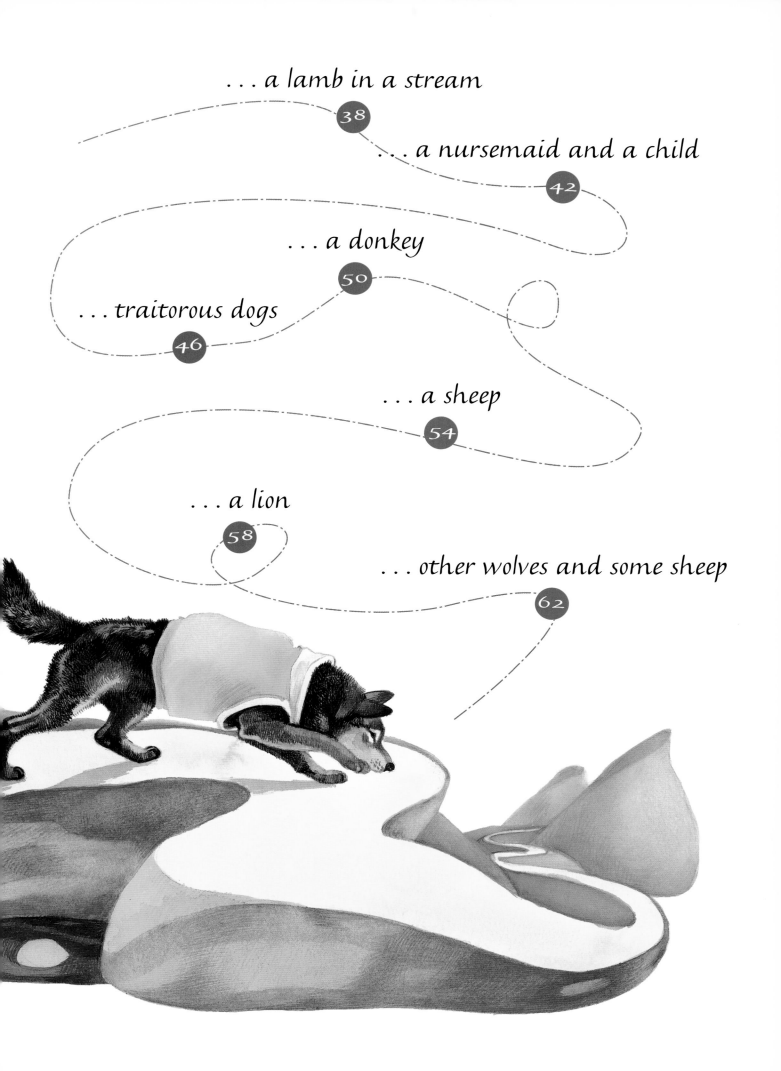

A wolf and . . .
a lamb in a stream

It was twilight and a lamb moved away from the flock to drink some water from a stream. He was drinking peacefully when, out of the corner of his eye, he saw a wolf quite a ways upstream from him, who was watching him while pretending that he was drinking too.

The wolf wished to find any way he could to devour the lamb and so accused him angrily.

"Lamb! Don't you realize that you are muddying the water I'm going to drink?"

"But I am only drinking with the tip of my tongue," answered the lamb. "And I don't know how you can say that, since I am downstream from you. If anything, it's you that is muddying my water!"

The wolf felt annoyed and spoke to the lamb in a nasty tone of voice.

"Yes, yes, I remember you now! You're the one who insulted my parents and my whole family last year!"

"But what are you saying? Last year I wasn't even born yet!" responded the lamb.

The wolf was now totally fed up with the way the lamb was answering and said to him in a fury:

"I realize, now, lamb, that you can find an excuse for everything. But don't think you are going to escape me. Soon you will be my supper!"

We must be careful and not get too close to danger,
or try to convince others whose objective is to do us harm.

A wolf and . . .
a nursemaid and a child

A wolf had not eaten for several days and was on the point of collapsing. He was dragging himself along, when, looking up, he saw he was approaching a house.

When he passed under one of the windows he heard a child crying and crying and the voice of a nursemaid trying to quiet him.

"Don't cry, don't cry, my baby, because if you keep on crying I will call the wolf!"

When the wolf heard what the nursemaid said he thought, "I'm going to wait until she calls me." And that was what he did. He stretched out under the window waiting for her to call him. He stayed there, without moving, until nightfall.

When it was dark, the wolf heard the nursemaid's voice again.
This time she was singing to the child in a soft voice.

"Sleep tight, my child, my pretty little one. If the wolf
comes we will kill him!"

At the sound of those words, the wolf set off running
and as he ran, leaving the house behind him, he said:

"They're all crazy at that house. First they say one thing,
then they say they want to do the opposite!"

The nursemaid in the fable told the child that she was going to do one thing and then assured him that she would do something else, to keep him safe forever. In true love, actions speak louder than words.

A wolf and . . .
traitorous dogs

A wolf, along with others from his pack, decided one day
to have a meeting with the dogs to reach an agreement
that would, of course, be in the interests of the wolves.

The wolf spoke to them in this way:

"Dear dogs, we are almost like brothers. We are like one another in almost every way, yet instead of treating each other well and loving one another we are always fighting! We have to change our attitude. The only difference I see between us is that we live in different ways. Wolves are free while dogs are submissive and always subject to men. Dogs always eat what their masters let them eat; wolves eat when they want. Men put collars and leashes on their dogs. Dogs are too faithful to their masters, and on top of that they guard their flocks and homes. There's a long list of obligations that dogs have and a long list of freedoms that we wolves enjoy. I want to make a proposal that will be advantageous for all dogs!"

And he continued:

"Why don't we join together, brothers? Why don't we take the flocks for ourselves once and for all and have a great feast together?"

The dogs let themselves be convinced by the wolves and thus betrayed the trust placed in them by their masters, who in fact had always taken care of them, fed them, and given them affection.

At night the wolves entered the pens that the dogs had left
unprotected, and the first thing they did was to kill all the dogs,
so that they could make off with the flocks more comfortably.

In this way the dogs were tricked into betraying their masters'
trust in them. We should not betray those who help us by
letting ourselves be fooled by others, because we will almost
always come out on the losing end.

A wolf and ...
a donkey

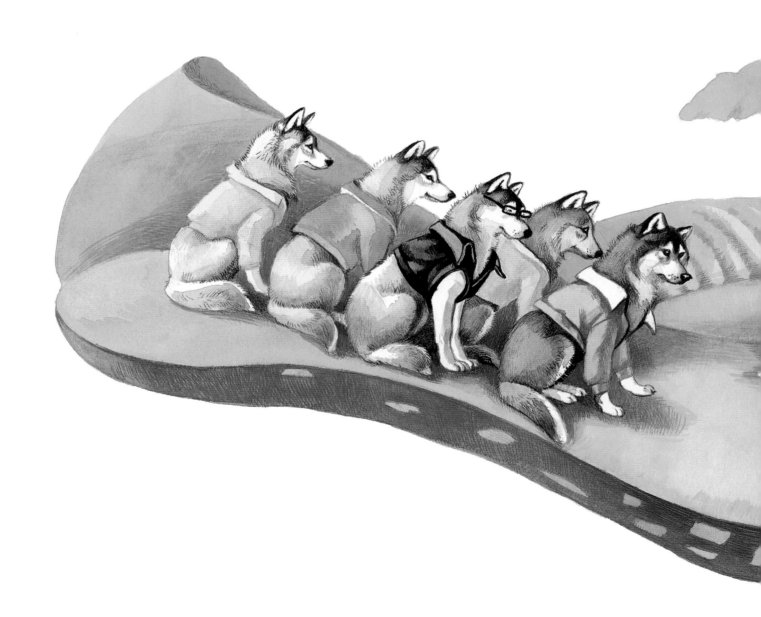

A large pack of wolves chose one of themselves to be head of the group. The first thing this wolf did when he took power was to order that each wolf should put the catch from his hunt into a big cave, where they would store everything together.

When it was time to eat they would all share the same amount, and when food was scarce they would still always have something to eat.

The wolf leader said:

"With this order no one will go hungry!"

But a donkey was walking by he heard the wolf's words.
He halted in front of him, began moving his big ears and said:

"I do not doubt, honest wolf, that this great idea that you have
had for all the wolves in your pack to live more comfortably
has come from the bottom of your heart, but then why do
you keep apart for yourself all that you catch? Take it to
the common cave like all the others, for that is why you
made this law"

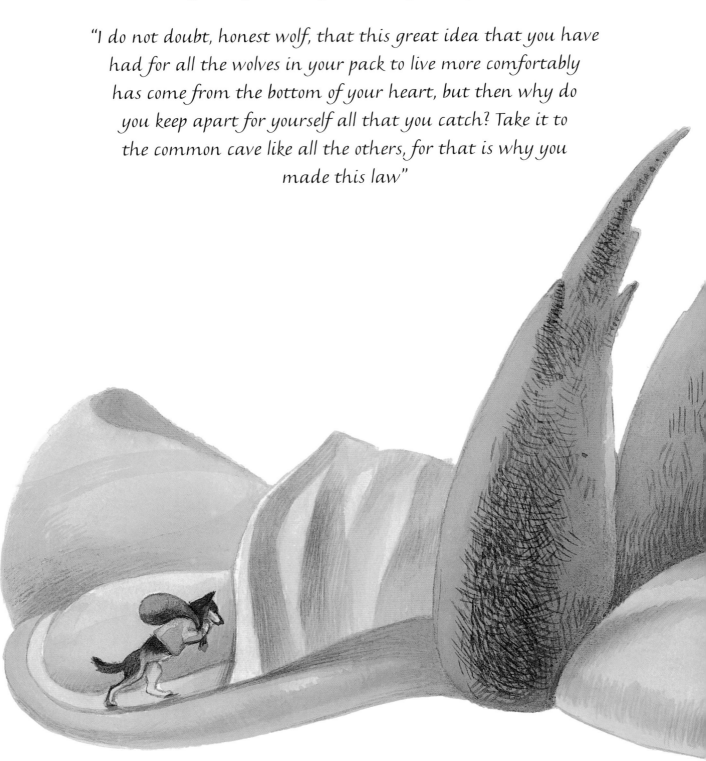

The wolf, having been found out, was ashamed of himself, and he abolished the law, so that each wolf again took care of this own food.

When you want someone to do what you say,
you must be sure that you are also ready to do the same.

A wolf and . . .
a sheep

A wolf was passing near a herd of sheep, and since he had recently eaten and was not hungry at all, he walked peacefully past them.

One of the sheep that was grazing there saw the wolf so very close to her and got terribly frightened and fell down in a faint.

The wolf realized that he had given the poor sheep the fright of her life and tried to revive her. When the sheep opened her eyes, the wolf said sweetly:

"Listen, sheep, I promise I will not touch a hair of your fleece if you tell me the three things you are thinking at this moment. I want the truth, though!"

The sheep answered him quickly enough.

"The first thing is that I would have preferred not to meet you. The second is that, since I did meet you, I wish you would have been blind. And the third . . . Look, I'll be sincere. I wish all you evil wolves would die in a terrible way! Because it isn't fair— we don't do anything to you, but you chase and kill us."

And having got all that off her chest, the sheep waited with drooping ears.

"Very good, sheep!" the wolf said. "You can go when you please, because your three thoughts are true, and very real at that!"

You must always go through life with a respect for the truth, even with people you are not fond of, because in the end the truth always wins out.

A wolf and . . .
a lion

One day at sunset a wolf was peacefully heading for his den.
He looked down at the ground and from side to side and
suddenly he saw his shadow, that was very long in
the afternoon sun. He looked enormous!

"What a great body I have! What size. There is no doubt but
that I can declare myself king of all the animals, since
I must be at least thirty yards long!"

The wolf felt very proud of himself and in that moment
he was only interested in his gigantic appearance and
his dreams of ruling over all the others.

But suddenly a hungry lion jumped on top of him, and after a few swipes of the lion's powerful claws, the wolf was on the point of death.

"Oh, poor me!" sobbed the wolf, "why did I have to be so vain, so proud. I would have been better off being careful of beasts that are fiercer than I am."

This proud wolf let himself be fooled by his own shadow. You should learn what qualities you really have and what your shortcomings are too.

A wolf and . . .
other wolves and some sheep

A wolf, who was the leader of the pack, proposed to
his companions that they send messengers to the herd
of sheep that they wanted to attack.

The wolves had been trying to kill some of the sheep for a long time but could not because the sheep dogs drove them off each time.

Finally the messengers managed to approach the sheep, and they said to them:

"We want to be your friends, but the dogs won't let us come near you. If you surrender them to us we can be your friends."

The sheep fell into the trap and forgot that the dogs were their guardians, who protected them and took them to the fields with the best grass and went looking for the lost lambs. They forgot all that and handed the dogs over to the wolves.

When the leader of the wolves and his pack saw that they were free of their enemies, they wasted no time in taking as prisoners the entire herd of sheep.

Never betray those who love us well. A friend is a treasure.

An eagle and . . .

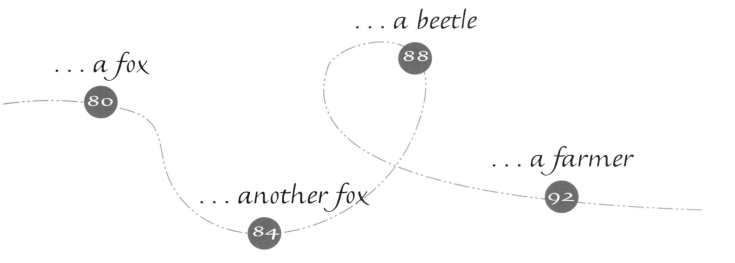

An eagle and . . .
a turtle

One warm day a turtle was enjoying the sun on a beach full
of seabirds. She watched them swirl and glide through the air,
dive into the water, and walk on their long, slim legs across
the sand and the rocks, and she began to complain.

"Oh, how sad my destiny is! How I would have liked to know
how to fly, but no one ever wished to teach me!"

An eagle gliding in circles through the air heard
her lament and made a proposal.

"Turtle, what will you give me if I take you high up into the sky?"

"I'll give you," replied the turtle, "all the riches of the Red Sea."

"Fine, fine," the eagle said. "In that case I shall teach you how to fly!"

The eagle took the turtle by her feet and carried her up as high
as the clouds. But suddenly she let go, just when they were
flying over a mountain range. The poor turtle's thick shell
was smashed to pieces when she hit the rocks.

Finding herself close to death, she complained again.

"This is what's happened to me for grumbling about my fate.
Why did it have to occur to me to want to fly, when I know
nothing of clouds and winds? Besides that, being a turtle,
I can scarcely drag myself along the ground!"

It is not good for us to desire something that we can never
hope to achieve. And also, if we get all we want too easily,
sooner or later we will usually be sadly disappointed.

An eagle and . . .
some roosters

Two big handsome roosters, one with reddish-colored feathers
and the other jet black, were locked in a terrible struggle,
because they both wanted to be king of the henhouse.

After a long hour of fighting the reddish-colored rooster gave up, while
the one with feathers of jet black, proud and victorious, flew up to the
very highest point of the wall and sang the news of his success to the
four corners of the world: "I am the kiiiinnng, I am the winnnnnerrr!"

An eagle who had been watching the fight from high
in the sky, seeing that the black rooster, so proud of himself,
was all alone on the wall, did not hesitate an instant
but swooped down upon him, grasped him in her claws,
and carried him off for her little ones to eat.

The rooster with the pretty red feathers,
who had watched the eagle's attack from the
corner of the henhouse, now strutted out into
the center and presented himself to the
hens as the new king.

"From this moment on,
I will be your king."

Do not brag about your successes, blinded by your own pride,
because someone or something may always appear
to take them away from you.

An eagle and . . .
a crow and a shepherd

One afternoon, when a shepherd was taking his sheep
back to the fold, an eagle that was watching them from
some high rocks nearby swooped down on a lamb and
snatched him up from his mother's side.

A crow saw what the eagle had done and wanted to do the same.
He flew down from the branch of a tree onto a ram, but since
he knew nothing of the eagle's way of doing things, his feet
got tangled up in the ram's fleece, and though he flapped his wings
with all his might he could not free himself and fly away.

The shepherd, who had seen all this, seized the crow, cut off the tips of his wings and gave him as a present to his children.

While they were playing with him, they asked their father a question.

"Papa, what kind of bird is this?"

And the father answered:
"For me he's just a crow, but he thinks he's an eagle."

Devote yourself to what you are really capable of doing. Know yourself first and then take good advantage of your abilities.

An eagle and . . .
a fox

An eagle and a fox had become friends and they decided that
now that they were going to have little ones, they would settle down
to live near one another.

The eagle chose a tall tree in order to be able to hatch her eggs
in a big nest, and the fox decided to have her young in
some bushes at the foot of her friend's tree.

The eagle had her eaglets and the fox her pups, and the
two neighbors congratulated one another on their good fortune.

But one morning, when the fox went out to look for food, the eagle woke
up hungry and so did her little ones. She felt too lazy to fly off that
morning, and looking down she saw that her friend's pups were all
alone. Without thinking twice, she swooped down upon them and
carried them up to her nest for a breakfast feast with her eaglets.

When the fox returned and discovered what the eagle had done,
her first thought was to avenge the death of her pups. But the fox
could not fly. How could she, an animal that walked on land, hunt
down another animal that knew how to fly? The poor thing had to
make do with barking insults at the eagle and her young.

However, not much time was to pass before the eagle
got what she deserved.

Some shepherds were roasting a lamb over an open fire for
their lunch when the eagle swooped down and carried off a big piece
of meat that was still burning between her claws.

Arriving at the nest, she dropped her prize into the middle of it so that
the whole family could enjoy it. But the flames from the burning piece
of meat set the nest on fire. Terrified, the eagle flew up into the air, but
the eaglets, who did not yet know how to fly, fell to the foot of the tree.

The fox came out of the bushes and, taking her time, well aware
that the eagle was circling in the sky above, watching her every move,
she ate the eaglets of her former friend one by one.

Do not betray sincere friendship, because in the end
you may often be the one that is betrayed.

An eagle and . . .
another fox

One day a man caught an eagle. He cut off the tips
of her wings and left her to run around the barnyard
with the roosters, hens, rabbits, and ducks.

With every passing day the eagle felt sadder and
more humiliated. She could not bring herself to eat or drink,
and she felt like a queen in prison.

Another man saw her and liked her and decided to buy her from
the owner. This new owner pulled out the feathers that had been cut,
and cared for the eagle until she had grown new feathers that were
strong and beautiful. When the eagle had recovered, she flew up into
the air. She caught the first hare she saw and carried it off to the
house of the man who had saved her to give it to him as a gift.

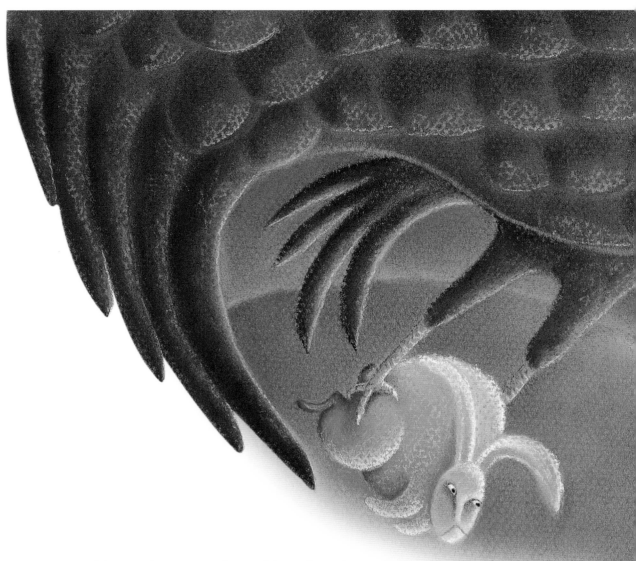

Along the way she told a fox about her plans,
and the fox, full of mischief, gave her some bad advice.

"Eagle, you silly thing, don't take the hare to the one who saved
you and set you free but to the other one, who took you prisoner.
The man who saved you is good and needs no gifts to make him
better. You should give the hare to the one who captured you to
make him kinder, so that he will never take you prisoner again."

The eagle did not, however, follow the fox's advice. She gave the hare
to the man who had saved her because she was grateful to him.

Be generous to those who do good things for you or give you their friendship, and pay no attention to those who tell you not to do that.

An eagle and . . .
a beetle

A hare was running desperately, pursued by an eagle
in the sky overhead. The poor hare knew she was lost and
asked a beetle that happened to cross her path for help.

The beetle begged the eagle to leave the hare alone,
but the eagle only laughed at the puny little beetle
and ate the hare right there in front of him.

From that day on the beetle, seeking revenge, followed the eagle
to her nest, where she guarded her eggs. The beetle rolled the eggs
out so that they fell to the ground, where they broke in pieces.
In this way he made sure that the eagle would have no little eaglets.

The eagle could find no solution to this problem except to appeal to
the gods, in particular the great god Zeus. She explained
her problem to him and asked him for a safe place to lay her eggs
and keep them safe until they hatched.

Zeus generously offered to keep them in his lap while
he was sitting down. And the eagle agreed to this.

But the beetle, seeing the eagle's plan, made a little ball of mud
and excrement, flew over Zeus's head, and dropped the ball
into the god's lap.

Startled, Zeus jumped up and shook his clothes, letting fall
all the eagle's eggs before he realized what he was doing.

For this reason eagles never lay eggs at the
time of year when the beetles fly.

Always be ready to help a worthy cause, as this beetle did,
and do not, like the eagle, despise those you think
are weaker than you, because you may well be surprised.

An eagle and . . .
a farmer

A farmer found an eagle caught in a trap, and she looked
so beautiful, with such clean feathers, her great wings spread wide,
with all her youth and liveliness confined in that horrible trap,
that he felt sorry for her and set her free.

Let no one believe that the eagle was ungrateful to her benefactor,
for one day she saw him sitting beside a wall that looked like
it was about to collapse, and, seeing the danger he was in,
she flew over the farmer's head and snatched off his hat.

The farmer, surprised, leaped up and raced after the eagle and
his hat, and when he was well away from the wall the eagle
dropped the hat from her claws so that the man could pick it up.

When the farmer was about to put his hat back on,
a terrible noise attracted his attention. The wall where
he had been sitting was crumbling to bits.

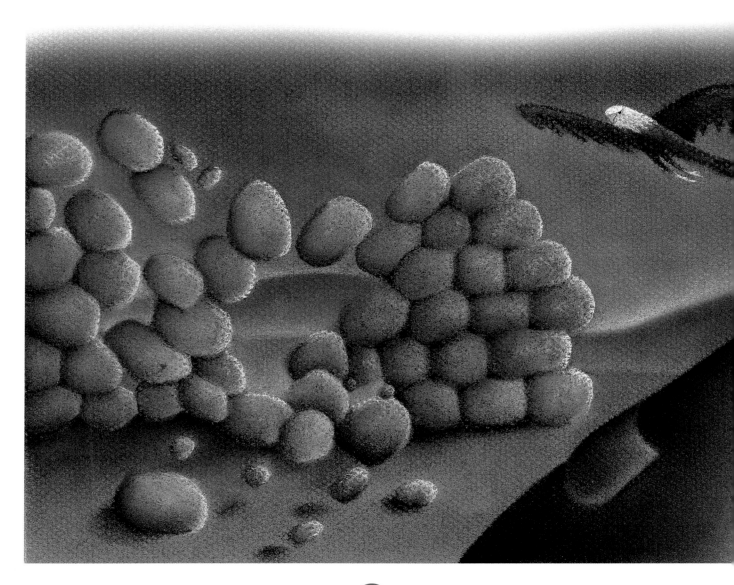

He realized then that the eagle had saved his life. Thus the eagle thanked him for what one day he had done for her.

We should always be grateful to those who do good to us.

A lion and . . .

. . . his reign of justice

118

. . . another mouse
and another fox

122

A lion and . . .

a mouse

A big lion was sleeping in the shade of a very old tree when
a field mouse climbed up his front legs and into the thick
of the King of the Jungle's long mane.

The little mouse played at swinging on the long hairs of the
lion's mane until finally the big cat opened his eyes and grabbed
the mouse with a swipe of his paw. The lion was about to gobble him
right up, and the frightened little animal begged for mercy.

"I'm sorry, I'm sorry. I had no wish to annoy
Your Majesty. I promise that if you let me go free, perhaps some day
you will need me and I will always be ready to help you."

The lion's laughter was so loud you could hear it
miles away, in all directions.

"How can you imagine that I am ever going to need
your help, you puny little thing? But, all right, you've
made me laugh and I'll let you go. Go on, get out of here!"

Not much time passed, however, before the King of the Jungle found himself caught in a trap. He was tangled in a net made of rope that some hunters had prepared because they wanted to capture him alive.

The lion roared pathetically, and by chance, the little mouse heard his voice and found the place where the great king lay helpless. The mouse recognized the lion and, without thinking twice about it, began gnawing at the ropes that held the lion fast, until he managed to set him free.

"A few days ago," he told the lion, "you laughed at me because you thought I could never do anything for you. But now you can see that we little mice keep our promises and sometimes we can also help the great animals of the jungle."

So the lion and the mouse swore to remain friends forever.

If you think someone is not as strong as you are and that you can laugh at them or pay them no attention because you will never need their help, you are very much mistaken. We all need each other sometimes, and that is why we should always help one another and never fail to keep our promises.

A lion and . . .
a cautious bull

This is the story of a lion who wanted to eat a bull
but kept running into difficulties in the matter.

One day it occurred to him that if he were going to achieve his aim
he would have to be sly, and so he decided to invite the bull to supper.

He told the bull that he had killed a ram and invited him to share it.
The lion's plan was to attack the bull when he sat down to eat.

When the bull arrived at the place where the lion lived, the first thing
he did was to take a good look around, paying close attention
to everything his host had prepared.

The bull observed, for example, that there were big platters and
casseroles around the fire and that the lion had set up an enormous
grill. He also noticed that there was no sign of a ram anywhere.
Once he had seen all that, he walked away without saying a word.

The lion called to him and asked him why he was going off like that, when he, the lion, had not done anything wrong. The bull turned toward him and answered:

"There is only one reason, 'friend'! All the preparations that you have made for this supper are not to cook or eat a ram, but to kill, cook, and eat a bull."

And from then on he did not want to even look at the lion.

Do you see how useful it is to observe, analyze, and think about everything around us? There is no better way to avoid all sorts of danger.

A lion and . . .
a hare

A hare was sleeping confidently in the weeds when a passing lion
saw her there. At the moment the lion was about to devour her,
a beautiful, delicate deer passed before his eyes. The lion left the hare,
who had woken up with a fright, and ran off after the deer.

The hare, seeing that she was free, ran as fast as
she could to get away from the danger.

Meanwhile, the deer ran faster than the King of the Jungle,
who eventually got tired, so tired that he decided to give up
the chase and go back to get the hare he had left behind.

When he reached the place he had left her he discovered that
the hare had run off, and he could not see her anywhere.
Then the lion realized how impulsive and foolish he had been.

"I deserve what I got, because I had my prize, and I let her escape
while I went after another one that was bigger but more difficult
and, in the end, impossible to catch. I was not at all wise!"

If you have something, do not give it up too soon for
something else that you have seen and would love to have,
because you might end up without either one.

A lion and . . .
a cocky mosquito

A mosquito was buzzing around the King of the Jungle's head.

"Do you think I'm afraid of you, lion?" she said in her buzzy voice.
"Well, I'm not. Do you perhaps believe that just because you
rip with your claws and bite and kill with your fangs
that you are stronger than I am? Don't believe it.
Look, let's have a battle, and you'll see who wins!"

And with a loud buzzing she flew down onto the lion's snout
and stung him on the nose, where the lion has no hair.

The lion, annoyed, began to scratch himself with
his own claws until he decided to call off the fight.

The mosquito gave a buzz of victory and, swirling and spinning through the air, without realizing it, she got tangled up in a spider's web.

The spider did not hesitate a second before attacking the mosquito, who cried out sadly while the spider ate her up.

"Oh, poor me! I, who have fought against the most powerful animals on Earth and beaten them, have let myself be killed by this insignificant creature, a spider."

Look where all her cockiness got the mosquito! Sometimes a person
is strong and succeeds at things that seem impossible, but that does not
mean that the person will always be the winner. At another time,
though you think the challenge is small, you may not succeed.

A lion and . . .
a donkey and a fox

One fine day, a lion, a donkey, and a fox decided
to go hunting together, as partners.

They had good hunting and brought down many prizes.

The lion told the donkey to divide up what they had,
so the donkey made up three equal parts and let the lion choose.

The lion, when he saw that his part was the same as that
of the other two, threw himself on the donkey and ate him up.

After that he told the fox to divide the results
of the hunt in two parts.

The fox put together the greater part of all they had hunted in one
pile and in the other she put only the scraps. When she had prepared
their two parts she called the lion and told him to choose.

The lion, quite satisfied with this,
of course took the bigger pile and turned to the fox.

"My dear colleague, who taught you to divide things up so well?"

And the fox answered through clenched teeth.

"None other than the donkey himself and what happened to him, sir!"

And with the scraps in her mouth, the fox rushed off
with her tail between her legs.

This fox was saved when she saw the mistake the donkey made, which cost him his life. She preferred not to fall into the same trap and risk her own.

A lion and . . .
his reign of justice

There was once a lion that never got angry and was never cruel or
violent. He was friendly, treated everyone well, and was always just,
and thus everyone thought that he was the most excellent
of all creatures. So all the animals named him king.

A few days after the beginning of his reign he brought together
all his subjects on a great grassy plain for them to make peace
and ask one another's forgiveness, so that from then on
they could all live together in harmony and justice.

The wolf made peace with the lamb, the panther and the tiger
begged the pardon of the deer and gazelles, the snakes made up
with the birds, the fox bowed to the hare, and so on and so forth.

But after the meeting was over the hare had this to say:

"I have always wished to see the coming of this day
of reconciliation and justice for all. A day on which
the weaker animals, like me, are treated with respect
and justice by those who are stronger and more powerful."

And almost before her speech was finished,
she took to her heels and ran.

The hare thought—and she was right—that she and all the other humbler
animals can live in peace where justice reigns, but common sense
made her cautious, and thus she did not want to stay too near.

A lion and ...
another mouse
and another fox

A lion was sleeping peacefully in the shade and a little mouse,
who was lost, started walking and running up and down
the whole of the King of the Jungle's body.

The lion opened one eye and then the other,
and began to shift and roll around on the grass
in search of the intruder that was annoying him.

Meanwhile a fox, observing the lion from a little mound, scolded him
for being afraid of a simple little mouse, while he was a great king.

"I'm not afraid of the mouse, you bold fox. I am just amazed that there could exist an animal who would dare to trod upon and scurry all over the body of a great sleeping lion."

The lion shook the mouse off and went on sleeping.

Consider how even the most powerful creatures, like the lion, must always pay attention to everything, even the most insignificant things.

GERMANO OVANI
Illustrator of "A fox and . . ."

Born in Pisaro, Italy, in 1970, he presently lives
in Edinburgh, Scotland, U.K.

From his home base there, he illustrates children's
and juvenile books for many publishers.

Since 1995, he has shown his works in various
Italian and British art galleries.

SIMONA BUCAN
Illustrator of "A wolf and . . ."

Born in Craiova, Romania, in 1967, she lives in Bucharest, Romania.
She was the illustrator selected for the 2003 Bologne Children
and Juvenile Book Fair exhibition.

She has studied painting, illustration, and graphic design in Bucharest.
She has taken courses in Lincolnshire College of Art and Design (Lincoln, U.K.).

She has received illustration, engraving, and design prizes in Romania and Turkey,
and was nominated for a prize in Bologne and at the Paris Book Salon in 1992.

Her works have been displayed in a number of places.

DANIELA PELLEGRINI
Illustrator of "An eagle and . . ."

Born in Pisaro, Italy, in 1975, where she still lives and
continues her professional activities.
For a number of years, she has regularly participated in courses and
workshops on painting, illustration, and other artistic disciplines under the
tutelage of reputed artists such as Giulano Ferri and Jozef Wilkon.

Her dedication to social work in a center for mentally handicapped people
has allowed her to experiment with art as a means of personal expression.
In this center, she coordinates workshops and other artistic activities.

Presently, she is part of an artist's group in Pisaro
that exhibits its works in different parts of the city.

MANUELA CENCI
Illustrator of "A lion and . . ."

Born in Rimini, Italy, in 1964, she graduated from the
Urbino Art Institute in 1983, where she specialized in graphic design.

For a number of years, she worked at various marketing agencies.
Beginning in 2000, she started work on her true passion:
illustration of children's books.

Since then, she has worked for a number of publishers, where she illustrates
books using mixed media, such as watercolors, inks, and pastels.

A fox and . . .

An eagle and . . .

A wolf and . . .

A lion and . . .

First edition for the United States, its territories and dependencies, and Canada published in 2006 by Barron's Educational Series, Inc.

© Copyright 2005 of English-language translation by Parramón Ediciones, S.A.

Original title of the book in Spanish: *Fabuloso Esopo*
© Copyright 2005 by Parramón Ediciones, S.A.–World Rights
Published by Parramón Ediciones, S.A., Barcelona Spain

Editorial Director: Jesús Araújo
Copy Editor: Elena Marigó
Selection and adaptation of text: Children's Division, Parramón Ediciones, S.A.
Proofreader: Esteve Pujol
Illustrators: Germano Ovani, Simona Bucan, Daniela Pellegrini, and Manuela Cenci
Graphic Designer: Álex Guerrero
Production Director: Rafael Marfil
Production Manager: Manel Sánchez

All inquiries should be addressed to:
Barron's Educational Series, Inc.
250 Wireless Boulevard
Hauppauge, NY 11788
www.barronseduc.com

ISBN-13: 978-0-7641-5930-5
ISBN-10: 0-7641-5930-5

Library of Congress Control Number: 2005929083

Printed in China
9 8 7 6 5 4 3 2 1